A Basket of Murder

A Pet Shop Mystery

Book Four

By

Susie Gayle

Copyright © 2017 Susie Gayle

All rights reserved.

ISBN: 9781542934664

Copyright 2017 Summer Prescott Books

All Rights Reserved*. No part of this publication nor any of the information herein may be quoted from, nor reproduced, in any form, including but not limited to: printing, scanning, photocopying or any other printed, digital, or audio formats, without prior express written consent of the copyright holder.*

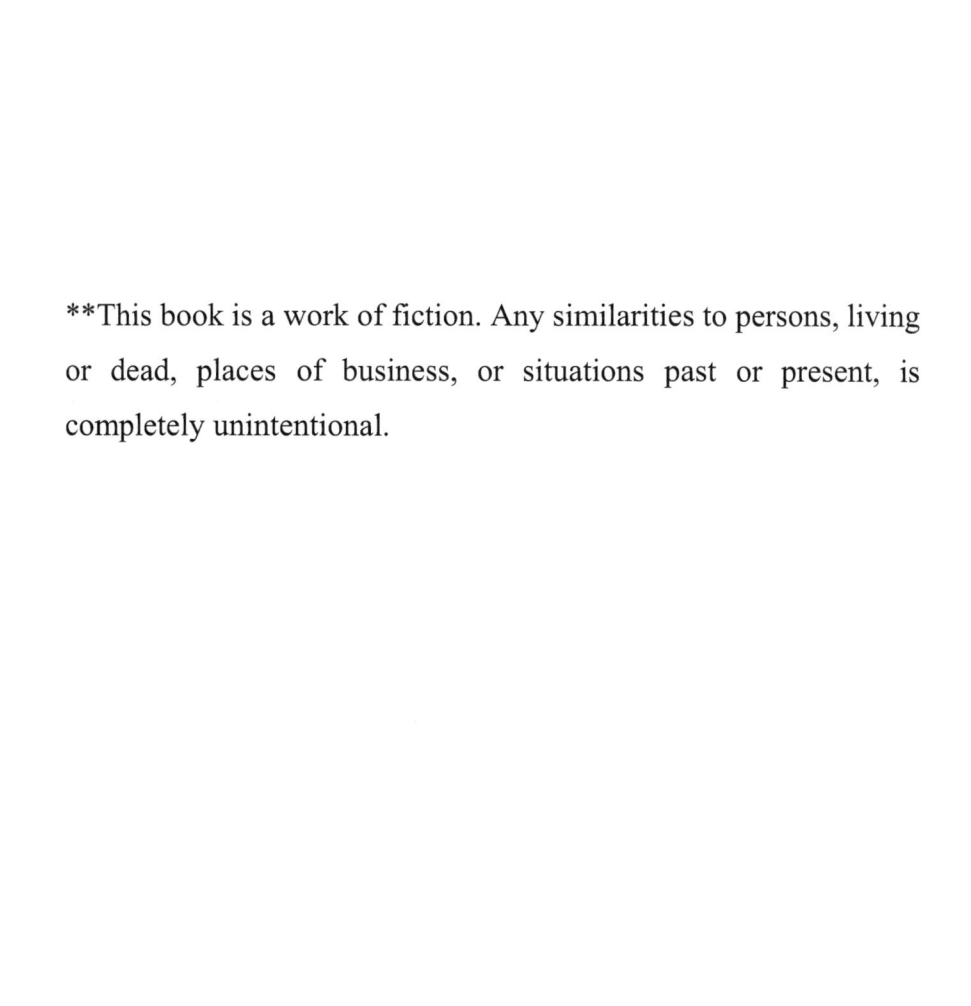

**This book is a work of fiction. Any similarities to persons, living or dead, places of business, or situations past or present, is completely unintentional.

Author's Note: On the next page, you'll find out how to access all of my books easily, as well as locate books by best-selling author, Summer Prescott. I'd love to hear your thoughts on my books, the storylines, and anything else that you'd like to comment on – reader feedback is very important to me. Please see the following page for my publisher's contact information. If you'd like to be on her list of "folks to contact" with updates, release and sales notifications, etc…just shoot her an email and let her know. Thanks for reading!

Also…

…if you're looking for more great reads, from me and Summer, check out the Summer Prescott Publishing Book Catalog:

http://summerprescottbooks.com/book-catalog/ for some truly delicious stories.

TABLE OF CONTENT

CHAPTER 1 9

CHAPTER 2 15

CHAPTER 3 22

CHAPTER 4 28

CHAPTER 5 36

CHAPTER 6 42

CHAPTER 7 48

CHAPTER 8 55

CHAPTER 9 61

CHAPTER 10 67

CHAPTER 11 74

CHAPTER 12 80

CHAPTER 13 86

CHAPTER 14 92

CHAPTER 15 99

CHAPTER 16 105

CHAPTER 17 112

A BASKET OF MURDER

A Pet Shop Mystery Book Four

CHAPTER 1

"Look, all I'm saying," Sarah tells me as I pull my SUV into the small parking lot behind the pet shop, "is you should just do it, instead of talking about it."

"But it's so hard," I whine. "I've been out of school for, what, sixteen years? What if I fail?"

She shrugs. "Then at least you can say you tried."

"Meh." I cut the engine and just sit there, drumming my fingers on the steering wheel. Behind me, Rowdy, my adopted furbaby and former shelter dog, groans and puts a paw over his face. We've been having this conversation for a while now; he's heard it all before.

See, over the past year or so, I've had something of a knack for getting involved in things I probably shouldn't, or being in the wrong place at the wrong time—and it just so happened that I sort of solved a couple of murders. The local chief of police, Patty Mayhew, slipped me a brochure about becoming a private investigator in Maine. Problem is, it requires sixty related course credits—of which I have zero.

"It would be over before you know it," Sarah insists. "And you have the time; the pet shop is doing just fine." That part is true. Sarah and I have been dating for the better part of a year, and she's been the only employee of my store, the Pet Shop Stop, for even longer. Recently I made her full-time and gave her a new title—Business Manager—and she took to it with gusto. Since then business has improved and sales have been up. In fact, outside of some bookkeeping and walking the dogs, I really haven't had to do much.

I sigh. So much has changed in only a few short months. Not only with the notion of going back to school and Sarah handling so much of the responsibility at the shop, but also in our personal lives. She's been staying over at my place, a rented house on Saltwater Drive, pretty frequently lately; days at a time. That's certainly no complaint on my part. Though I have to admit that the first time I saw the pink toothbrush sitting on my bathroom sink, it weirded me out a little.

I'm by no means afraid of commitment—I was married once before, for seven years, but it ended badly. So I feel somewhat justified in taking things slower this time around.

Anyway, it started with a toothbrush, and soon it was a Sarah drawer in my bureau. Then her favorite coffee mug was in my cupboard, and soon after, she bought a new set of bed sheets—mine were apparently an embarrassingly low thread-count—that she referred to as *our* sheets. What all this is culminating in, if I had to guess, is that Sarah is wondering when we're going to take this relationship to the next level. You know what they say; we're not getting any younger. (Which, by the way, is about the poorest excuse for anyone anywhere to do anything, ever.)

"Will, I don't want you to feel pressured to do anything," she says, putting her hand on mine. I look up sharply and her too-green eyes bore into mine. Is she reading my mind? No; she's talking about the classes. "If you're not comfortable doing it, then don't do it. It should be what *you* want." At least I'm pretty sure she's still talking about the classes.

"I just need more time to think about it," I tell her. "Come on; let's open the shop."

The three of us—me, Sarah and Rowdy—get out of the car and head around to the front of the building. The Pet Shop Stop isn't very large, or even all that impressive, but I like it that way. It's a fairly unassuming little place on Center Street in downtown Seaview Rock, our charming coastal town. Most of our business comes from residents, local pet owners that need supplies regularly. Sure, they could go to Sprawl-Mart just outside of town, or twenty-five minutes down the highway where the nearest big-box pet store is, but people around here are real good about supporting small businesses.

The other part of our patronage we get from tourism, weekend road-trippers that come to see our delightful seaside town. Seaview Rock used to be a tiny fishing village until a few hatcheries opened up and the area blossomed in the mid-nineteenth century. Almost all of the architecture in town has remained in the style of that era, and we work pretty hard to keep our streets and shoreline clean, all of which makes it very alluring for folks to stop by for a visit.

And it's because of those folks (who tend to be impulse buyers) that we keep a veritable menagerie of animals—pups, kittens, chinchillas, ferrets, rabbits, guinea pigs, hamsters, gerbils, turtles, parakeets, some small colorful fish, and a handful of lizards.

But not snakes. Never snakes. If there are two things I have in common with Indiana Jones, it's that I don't care for snakes, and I look darn good in a Stetson.

As we're rounding the corner toward the building, Rowdy sniffs the air twice and bounds ahead of us. Sarah and I exchange a glance; Rowdy's a smart dog and I've trained him to walk well off-leash, so him getting excited over something and running ahead is cause for at least mild concern.

We hurry after him and find him just outside the door to the pet shop, his nose buried in a wicker basket, sniffing deep breaths as he pokes his snout around a tiny blue blanket.

"What is that?" Sarah wonders aloud.

I gently pull Rowdy away by the collar as Sarah picks up the basket, lifts the blanket, and gasps.

"What is it?"

She looks up at me with her eyes wide. Then she reaches in and takes out a very tiny ball of fluff.

Her face lights up in an enormous smile. "It's a kitty!"

SUSIE GAYLE

CHAPTER 2

I unlock the door to the pet shop and we bring the poor little thing inside out of the cold. For a lot of places, late March signals the end of winter and the first signs of spring. Not in coastal Maine.

She sets the basket down on the counter and searches it for any contents other than the blanket and cat. "There's no note or anything."

"Weird. Why would someone bring it here, and not the shelter?" Our local animal shelter, which Sarah volunteers at a couple times a week, is pretty great as far as shelters go. They're no-kill, and they actively seek adoption outlets rather than the other way around.

She holds the tiny kitten aloft and peers at it. "Well, first of all, he can't be more than two or three weeks old," she says. "Maybe whoever left him here thought we'd take better care of him."

The little kitten is gray and his eyes, though tiny and squinting, are a bright blue. I notice something else about him, too.

"Sarah, look." I point out one of his hind paws—or lack thereof. The kitten only has three feet.

"Oh my god! The poor thing. You think he was in an accident or something?"

"No," I say slowly, inspecting the missing paw. "Looks like he was born without it."

She turns to face me and bats her eyelashes a few times and I know what's coming next.

"Sarah," I tell her gently, "we can't—"

"What should we call him?"

"Oh, please don't name him." Look, I love animals, big and small. (Even snakes—I just love them from a safe distance.) But as soon as she names him, I know exactly what's going to happen: one, she's going to get attached. And two, that little kitten won't be going anywhere.

"Let's call him Basket!" she says.

And there it is.

"Sarah, listen. You can't have pets at your place, and I'm not home enough to take care of a baby kitten. And we both know I can't rightfully sell this cat without knowing where it came from. The only thing to do here is to bring him to the shelter. You know them; they'll take good care of him."

"That's where you're wrong. There is another option. He could be our temporary little shop-cat."

"Sarah…"

"But he's just a baby," she says, staring into the kitten's little blue eyes. "He can't even eat solid food yet. He needs love and attention."

"I don't think that's a good idea—"

"Fine," she says, and she turns the kitten to face me. "Then you tell him that. Tell him we refuse to keep him around, even if just for a little while, and feed him and take care of him and love him." She looks at me sternly, holding the hapless three-legged kitten aloft. "Go ahead. Tell him how cruel the world is. He's waiting."

"I..." Ugh. That's totally not fair. "Alright, alright. Jeez. We'll keep him around—just for a few weeks, until he's eating solid food and okay on his own."

"Yay!" Sarah gently puts the cat back in the basket and throws her arms around my neck. Then she hurries over to the shelves of cat supplies. "Alright, we'll need a little bed, and a bottle, and kitten milk..."

I glance down at the tiny beast. "Basket, huh?" He looks up at me and yawns, punctuating it with a tiny squeak. "And what do you think of all this?" I ask Rowdy, sitting near my feet. He groans and retreats to his own bed, behind the counter. "Yeah. Me too, buddy."

*   *   *

After the unexpected arrival of Basket, the rest of the day is fairly ordinary. Almost every customer that comes in is utterly delighted by the ridiculously cute cat that Sarah carries around almost nonstop, either cradling him in an arm as she feeds him from a bottle or tucking him into the large pocket in the front of her apron.

It doesn't take long to discover that every time Basket yawns—which is a *lot*—he lets out a tiny little squeak, which prompts Sarah to squeal and say, "Will! He did it again!"

By the end of the day I am very much aware that we now have a shop-cat, and that there's a very high probability that Basket isn't going anywhere.

Eight o'clock is normally quitting time, so as we're doing our closing duties—feeding the animals, making sure they have water, sweeping the floor—I ask Sarah what she wants to do for dinner. We usually end up eating pretty late on weekdays, on account of only being two of us to run the shop.

Sarah purses her lips and glances at the floor. "Sorry, I forgot to tell you. I have, uh, plans tonight."

"You do?" I don't mean it to sound like Sarah doesn't have a life beyond me, though it sort of comes out that way.

"Yeah. I'm going out with the girls."

"The girls?" I don't mean it to sound Sarah doesn't have friends beyond me, though it sort of comes out that way. "I've never heard you refer to anyone as 'the girls.' Who are these girls?"

"You know," she says casually. Then she adds quietly, "Anna... and Karen."

I actually drop the broom in my hands and it clatters to the floor. "You're going out with my ex-wife?"

She shoots me a sidelong glance. "Don't be so melodramatic. It's not a big deal. We've been talking, and…"

"You've been talking?"

"Yes, Will. Talking. Like grown-ups do. Anyway, we decided to try that new Mexican place together, Holy Frijole. I hear they have great margaritas…"

"Hang on. I'm still processing this."

She scoffs. "Process away. I've got to go." She retrieves her purse from behind the counter, unzips it, and dumps the contents next to the cash register.

"Oh no, Sarah, please don't—"

Too late. Basket the shop-cat is now Basket the purse-cat.

"What?" she says. "I can't leave him here alone tonight." The tiny kitten's head peeks out from the top of her purse. He yawns and squeaks, and she giggles. "Why don't you call up Sammy and go to the Runside?"

"Yeah," I murmur. "That sounds good." What I really mean is, a Whale of an Ale sounds good right now. "You know, that cat is going to think you're its mother."

She thinks for a moment. "Well, maybe I will be." She hangs her apron on a hook, pulls on her jacket, and carefully shrugs the purse onto her shoulder. "I'll see you tomorrow morning." She gives me a kiss and heads out the door.

I pick up my broom and finish sweeping, thinking all the while. Sarah and Karen, hanging out? Doing things together? Being… friends? Will they talk about me? Oh my god… will they compare notes?

In my mind's eye, I can imagine them at a table, drinking margaritas and sharing nachos, Karen saying how I used to wear socks to bed because my feet get cold, and then Sarah laughing, telling her that I still do that.

What a nightmare.

I shake the thoughts from my head and take off my apron. "Come on, Ro-Ro," I call to Rowdy. "Let's go to the Runside."

A BASKET OF MURDER: A PET SHOP MYSTERY BOOK FOUR

CHAPTER 3

The Runside Bar & Grill is to Seaview Rock as the Cheers bar is to Boston. No offense to any wine sippers or margarita admirers, but if you're a home-brewed-beer kind of person, or a straight-no-chaser sort, the Runside is where you'd be. It helps that they serve up fresh seafood, too, caught by the owner's son by taking a short walk to the next-door pier.

On my way over, I call up Sammy Boy, my best friend, my confidant, the Banquo to my Macbeth (first-act Banquo, of course). Sammy owns and operates a small barber shop in town, the old-school sort that smells like talcum powder and shaving cream. He's unrivaled in the empathetic listening department, so naturally I can't wait to bend his ear about this latest development.

"Hey!" he says loudly into the phone. There's some noise in the background, a lot of chatter.

"Hey yourself. I'm heading to the Runside."

"Perfect! We're already here. See you soon." He hangs up.

We? Who's we? Looks like I might have an audience for my woes.

Look, some people might think I'm overreacting—and maybe I am. The truth is, Karen and I were married for almost seven years, during which I opened the Pet Shop Stop. I was the sole employee of a burgeoning business, so yeah, I worked a lot. She thought I cared more about the animals than I did her, and in order to get my attention, went and had an affair with some guy from Portland.

She got my attention, and a divorce, too. That was about four years ago. Turns out the guy she left me for went and had an affair on *her*, prompting her to move back to Seaview Rock. And if all of that isn't awkward enough, just a few short months ago Karen was the prime suspect in a murder case and Sarah, my Sarah, went and bailed her out. It seems that since then they've been talking. And now they're getting enchiladas together.

Like I said, a lot has changed in just a few short months.

"Relax," I tell myself aloud. "We're all mature adults. No reason we can't be civil." But then I remind myself that when Karen first came back to Seaview Rock, I did try to be civil—and she responded by trying to break Sarah and me up.

"Past is the past, though," I say. "Right, Rowdy?"

He lets out a little grunt from the backseat behind me.

When I get to the Runside, the place is packed—I forgot it was Thursday, dollar-draft night. I spot Sammy at a small round table near the rear, seated with two other familiar faces.

"Hey, guys," I greet them as I take a seat.

"Will's here!" one of the other two guys, Tony, throws his hands up. I guess he's already had a few. "How you doin', pal?" He claps me heartily on the back.

"Tony, Jerry, nice to see you." Tony and Jerry are a couple of mechanics that work at the local auto repair shop, Sockets & Sprockets. They're also Runside regulars, usually coming right from the shop and showing up in their gray grease-spattered jumpsuits—as they are on this occasion.

Tony is a stocky guy with a bushy black mustache. He's originally from Staten Island, which means he talks with his hands a lot and leaves off the "h" when he says "hey" (so it's like, "Ey!"). Jerry, on the other hand, is laid-back and soft-spoken. He's a couple years older than me, about to hit the big four-oh—which we like to taunt him about whenever the chance comes up—but he takes it with a smile and a shrug.

"Will, perfect timing," Sammy tells me. "Tony here was just asking about what it's like to run your own business."

"Oh? Are you thinking about striking out on your own?" I ask Tony. Then I cup a hand to my mouth and say in a stage whisper, "Should you be saying that in front of the competition?" I jerk a thumb towards Jerry, which gets a laugh.

"Nah, nothing like that," Tony says. "The old man wants to franchise Sockets & Sprockets, open a couple more locations. I figure I can get a piece of that; run my own shop." By "the old man" he means Mr. Casey, who owns the auto shop and the adjacent gas station.

Holly, the proprietor and bartender of the Runside, brings me a Whale of an Ale (what can I say? They know me here) and puts down a small bowl of water for Rowdy, patting him on the head as he lays partially beneath the table at my feet.

"Thanks, Holly." To Tony I say, "Well, it's a lot of work. You'll need a lawyer on retainer and a good accountant. You have to track expenses, pay employees, take care of all your taxes. Then there's advertising, paying rent and utilities, equipment costs…"

Tony waves a hand in the air. "No biggie. I got it all figured out. Besides, I've been saving up for a long while now. No more nine-to-five for this guy. I wanna be the boss, you know?"

"How about you, Jerry?" I ask. "Are you thinking of doing the same?"

"Oh, no. Not me," he says with a small smile. "I'm fine where I'm at."

"Yeah, this guy likes gettin' up at the crack of dawn and working for somebody else," Tony scoffs. "Just a regular good ol' boy, aren't you, Jerry?"

"I've got plenty going on already," Jerry says quietly. Sammy glances over at him, and for the briefest of moments I see an eyebrow raise and a half-smile, some sort of strange exchange between them. "Besides," Jerry adds, "I think I'm getting too old to go changing my whole lifestyle."

"That's definitely true," I say.

"Be retiring real soon, huh?" Sammy adds.

"Practically one foot in the grave," Tony chimes in.

Jerry chuckles and checks his watch. "Alright fellas, I got to get going. I told Carla I'd take a look at Garrett's car tonight before she got home. I'll see you around, huh?" He shrugs into his jacket, tosses a twenty on the table and heads out.

"Guess I should get ramblin', too," Tony remarks. "The wife gets cranky if she doesn't get her pre-bedtime foot rub." He grins and rises, and in a few moments it's just me and Sammy left at the table.

"What was that about?" I ask him.

"What was what about?"

"You and Jerry. That weird, furtive look. I saw that."

Sammy shrugs. "It was nothing. Guy's just got a lot going on. He's pushing forty with a live-in girlfriend and her eighteen-year-old son that hates him. Can you imagine?"

"I guess that is a lot," I murmur—because yes, I can imagine at least half of that scenario. "Speaking of, let me tell you what I found out today."

"Uh-oh," Sammy says with a smile. "Sounds like we might need another round for this one." He waves to Holly for another couple of pints.

A BASKET OF MURDER: A PET SHOP MYSTERY BOOK FOUR

CHAPTER 4

"Who's the world's most adorable little kitty? You are! You're the world's most adorable little kitty!" The next morning, Sarah paces the length of the shop floor as she cradles Basket in one arm, bottle-feeding him with the other.

Nearby, I stack bags of dog food for a sale and shake my head, grinning. I've caved to the notion of having a shop-cat, and instead decided to just find the humor in it.

"So," I say, clearing my throat. "How was girls' night out?"

"Oh, it was good," Sarah tells me. "But Anna couldn't make it—some work emergency—so it was just me and Karen."

My heart skips a beat. Just the two of them?

"That place has really good *queso* dip, by the way." She glances over at me, and I assume I've gone a shade paler because she half-smiles and asks, "So what did Sammy say about it?"

"Huh?"

"Come on, Will. He's your BFF. I know you talked to him about it. And he probably offered some words of wisdom, as usual. So, what'd he say?"

She's right, as she tends to be. "Well, Sammy said that I need to understand that people have a capacity to change, and that I should give Karen the benefit of the doubt. He also said that my perception of women as chatty and having nothing better to talk about than me is mildly sexist, and I need to get over that."

"Hmm. Wise as ever." She winks at me and adds, "But we totally talked about you."

"Wait, what? What'd you say? What'd *she* say? Sarah, come back!"

She laughs and paces to the rear of the store. At the same time the front door opens, and as I turn to greet what I assume is a customer, instead I see Sammy.

"Hey, speak of the devil..." I trail off. His normally coifed black hair is mussed, and his eyes are wide in alarm. "What's up? Something wrong, Sammy?"

"Will, I need to talk with you," he says urgently in nearly a whisper.

I glance left and right. There are no other customers in the store and Sarah's out of earshot. "Okay... What is it?"

"Will," he rubs his face with both hands and says, "Jerry Brahms is dead."

"What?! How?"

"He was found late last night in his garage," Sammy tells me. "But that's not the worst part of it." He lowers his voice even further, to the point I can barely hear him, and adds, "I'm sure it was murder."

"Whoa, hey. Slow down a second, pal. I don't even know what's going on—"

"Hey, Sam!" Sarah says brightly, approaching us. "Have you met Basket, the world's most precious little kitten?"

"I have not yet," Sammy says, his demeanor suddenly changing to a hearty smile. "Wow, look at him. That is a ridiculously adorable cat. Listen, Sarah, you mind if I borrow Will for just a few minutes? I need help moving something at the barber shop."

Now *that's* especially weird. I've never heard Sam lie to anyone, least of all Sarah.

"Not at all," she says. "Take him."

"Great. Back in a flash."

I grab my coat and follow Sammy outside.

* * *

I walk quickly to keep up with Sammy, who digs his hands into his coat pockets and lowers his head as he talks a mile a minute.

"So here's what I know. Jerry went home to work on Garrett's car—that's Carla's kid. The garage door was open. He had the back tires off. Carla came home close to midnight and found him. Now, what *looks* like happened is that the jack tipped and the wheel well crushed him. But I don't think that's what happened at all. Jerry's been a mechanic for almost twenty years; no way he'd get lazy about jacking up a car. I think someone waited until he was directly under the wheel well, and then jostled the car or did something to sabotage the jack." He looks over at me, his eyes wide. "Are you listening?"

"Yeah, I am." To be honest, I'm still stuck at the part where he said "Jerry's dead," but I don't mention that. "Sam, how do you know all this already?"

"Because I went to Jerry's house last night—"

"You were *there*?"

"Yes, but for something completely unrelated—"

"What reason would you have for going to Jerry's house at midnight? Couldn't you just have called him?"

"Look," Sammy says sharply, "the reason I was there isn't important. What's important is that the cops were already there when I got there. I saw it all with my own eyes. Then Patty told me to go home."

"Did *she* ask you why you were there?"

"I told her I was driving by and saw the flashers. Got curious. Look, we're getting off track. The point is, I believe Jerry was murdered, and…" He stops walking and stares me in the eye. "I want you to look into it."

"Look into it," I repeat.

"Yes. You have to admit, you're pretty keen on figuring out these kinds of things and—"

"Whoa, wait. Sam, I'm not getting mixed up in this. The police will handle it, I'm sure."

"The police don't know everything," he says simply. "Jerry and I were good friends. We hung out at the Runside together. We played racquetball at the rec center. I've known him for years. I don't think this was an accident at all."

"You're kind of freaking me out here. Do you know something that might be important about this?"

"I can't say."

"But you believe it's murder."

He nods. "So will you?" His eyes plead with mine. "I'm asking as your friend—as your *best* friend."

I think for a long moment, and then I shake my head. "No, Sammy. I'm sorry, but unless you can give me more to go on, I can't just assume it's murder and interfere. That's illegal, and I have nothing to do with it, and—"

"I think I might be next," he says suddenly.

"*What?* Why on earth would you think that? Why would there even be a 'next'?"

"I'm sorry, Will, but I—"

"You can't tell me."

"No."

"Sammy, what the heck are you mixed up in?" I sigh heavily. "Alright, so what if this turns out to have just been an accident?"

He shrugs. "That's the best-case scenario. I'd have nothing to worry about. But I wouldn't get your hopes up. I think someone tried to make this look like an accident."

"So you think it was murder, and you have reason to believe—reason that you can't tell me—that you might be a target for the next 'accident.'"

"That's right."

"Sammy, you understand this sounds crazy, right?"

"I know it does."

I groan. "Alright, let me just digest all this for a little bit, okay?"

"And then you'll look into it?" he asks eagerly.

"I… will look into it as far as I can without getting myself into any trouble," I tell him.

"Thanks, Will. Thank you. You're a good friend." He gives me a brief hug. "I have to get back to the shop. We'll talk later, okay?"

He hurries off down the street, hands plunged into his pockets and head low, while I run the strangest conversation I've ever had over in my mind. Why can't Sammy tell me what he knows? Why was he at Jerry's house so late at night?

If nothing else, Sammy's definitely piqued my curiosity—as much as I hate to admit it.

I walk slowly back to the Pet Shop Stop. Almost as soon as I enter, Sarah looks over at me with her brow furrowed in concern.

"You okay?" she asks. "You didn't hurt your back, did you?"

"What? Hurt my back…?"

"Helping Sammy."

"Oh. No, uh, it was a piece of cake." Wait, what am I doing? I'm not getting in the habit of lying now. "Sarah, he didn't need help moving anything. He needed to talk."

"Everything okay?"

"No. Not even a little bit." I tell her all about the conversation we just had and Sammy's odd behavior. At the end of it, I expect a flurry of questions—much in the same way I reacted to it—but instead Sarah asks only one.

"Well, you're going to help him, right? I mean, he's your best friend. He's always been there for you."

"Yeah," I mutter. "Of course I'm going to help him."

A BASKET OF MURDER: A PET SHOP MYSTERY BOOK FOUR

CHAPTER 5

I decide that the first move on the part of "reluctantly investigating pet shop owner" should be to talk to the police. Not only have I known Chief Mayhew personally for years, but she's the one that gave me the information about becoming a PI, after helping out on not one, but three different murder cases over the last year or so.

So just a couple hours after Sammy's visit, once I'm certain that everything is in order with the shop and that I'm not heaping too much responsibility on Sarah's shoulders, I head downtown to the police station to have a chat with my good friend Patty.

"What do you want, Sullivan?" she asks me when I knock gently on the frame of her open office door.

"Hey, Chief. Good to see you. You're looking especially vibrant this morning."

Truth be told, she looks tired as all get-out. She glances up at me from her paperwork without actually lifting her head. "Close the door."

I gulp and do so. As is her custom, she folds her hands on the desk between us before she starts speaking.

"Seaview Rock has always been a very nice place to live," she tells me. "Our crime rate, over the last eight years since I've been chief, has been astonishingly low. But now, for whatever reason, we're looking at our fourth murder inside a year. And each time, you've been nearby. That's a little disconcerting, right?"

"I could see how one might think so," I say carefully.

"Now here we seem to have another one, and lo and behold, Will Sullivan is nowhere around! A miracle, right?"

"You're right. Nowhere to be found."

"Yet... here you are."

I force a smile. "Here I am."

"So what do you want, Will?"

What I really want, if I'm being honest with myself, is for the police to have found evidence that Jerry's death was just a tragic accident. What I really want is to tell Patty that I plan to look into his death and for her to adamantly refuse, and to threaten to lock me up if I get involved. I know, it sounds like I'm being a bad friend, but I still can't help but think that the best course of action is to let the police handle it.

"I admit that I don't know a lot about the circumstances of Jerry's death," I say, choosing my words carefully. "But I have reason to believe that it might possibly have been murder."

The chief stares at me blankly. "Yeah. We know."

"Oh. You do?"

"Yes, Will. Believe it or not, the police are capable of solving things without you traipsing around."

"Traipsing? I don't traipse. If anything, I plod. Sometimes I schlep—"

"Look, I know that you guys liked to hang out and drink at the Runside, so if you think you're going to solve this guy's murder, I can tell you confidently that we've got it handled. If you're fishing for information, I can only tell you what I've already told the media."

"Sure, shoot." Any info is better than no info, and hopefully whatever Patty can tell me will satisfy Sammy.

"Alright. We already have someone in custody," she says.

"You do?"

"We have reason to believe that there was foul play. A dent in the rear fender near the wheel well of the car Jerry was working on suggests that it was kicked, and that it caused the jack to tip and the car to fall on him. The wheel well severed his spine; he died instantly. The only person that was home at the time was Garrett Kunkle, the son of Jerry's girlfriend. It's no secret that Garrett disliked Jerry, and the kid has some priors; he's been in and out of this station more than you have in the past year. So we're holding him under suspicion of murder."

"Oh!" I exclaim. "But... he's just a kid."

"He's eighteen, which by definition means he's not a kid."

I furrow my brow, thinking. I mean, on the one hand it seems awfully open-and-shut. But on the other hand, it feels... too easy.

"So that's it then?" I ask her. "You have your guy, cased closed?"

"Of course not. We still have to do our due diligence of finding hard evidence or getting a confession out of him—and Garrett has clammed up. His original statement is that he fell asleep in his room listening to music, and never heard a thing. His mom woke him up after she got home and found Jerry in the garage. Since he told us that, he hasn't said a word."

"And no one saw anything? No neighbors or passers-by?"

"No. It was pretty late at night; estimated time of death is around ten p.m. Carla got home around midnight and called us right away. Why, what are you thinking, Will?"

"I don't know. It just doesn't feel right to me."

She chuckles. "It doesn't feel right? You've gained an investigative intuition after all your *vast* experience?"

I roll my eyes. She's not wrong, though.

"Alright, Will. This is the part where I tell you not to get involved, and don't go sniffing around where you shouldn't, et cetera."

There's what I was looking for—an out. What a good friend I am, right?

"Well, I certainly wouldn't want to get on your bad side, Chief. You got it; I'll stay far away from all of this. Have a great afternoon." I rise and head for the door.

With my hand on the knob, the chief says, "Oh, Will?" Without even looking up from her paperwork, she says, "Let me know what you find."

I gulp. "Sure thing, Chief."

A BASKET OF MURDER: A PET SHOP MYSTERY BOOK FOUR

CHAPTER 6

Right after the chief's strange and confusing warning that wasn't really a warning, I get back into my car and immediately call Sammy. He answers on the third ring, and I tell him about my meeting with Chief Mayhew.

"I don't believe it for a second," Sammy insists. "Garrett isn't the world's greatest kid, and he definitely wasn't Jerry's biggest fan, but to kill the guy?"

"What if it was an accident? What if Garrett only meant to hurt Jerry, and not kill him?" I suggest.

"Come on, Will. You don't drop a car on a guy and hope to just hurt him a bit."

Well, he's got a point.

"Regardless," I say, "the chief told me to stay away from it."

There's silence on the other line for a few moments as Sammy thinks. "Did she say that you couldn't... offer your condolences to Carla?"

I sigh. "No. She didn't say that. I guess I'll go there next."

"Thanks, Will, you're the best." He sighs. "It's Friday. Me and Jerry used to play racquetball on Friday. Anyway, I'll talk to you later."

Once I end the call with him I ring Sarah at the shop and fill her in on the details. It usually helps to run things past someone like her, because she thinks of the things I don't.

"There's one thing I don't get," she says, coming through just as I'd hoped. "If Garrett did it, why would he just go upstairs to his room and pretend to be asleep—or worse, actually go to sleep? It would take a real sociopath to do something like that. I would think that a normal person would flee the scene, go somewhere public... try to establish an alibi."

"That's an excellent point," I tell her. "But we don't know enough about Garrett to make that assumption."

"True. What's next?"

"I'm going to talk to Carla and see if there's anything at all that she can add that might help. Sometimes people don't know what they know, you know?"

"Call me after."

"I will." I hang up my cell phone and start the car to head over to Jerry's house.

*   *   *

Jerry lived in a yellow split-level on the west side of town, within walking distance from the edge of Seaview Rock. I remember him being particularly proud that he managed to retain the house in the wake of his divorce a few years earlier. (Some guys get all the luck. When I split with Karen, she got the house and promptly sold it to pay for her place in Portland.) I wonder what will happen to it now, considering that he and Carla were only dating.

I park about a half a block away, but even from here I can see Carla's car at the bottom of the driveway, and beyond it, the open garage door cordoned off with yellow caution tape. The garage is empty; Garrett's car must have been towed to the police impound lot.

I take a deep breath, get out of the car and head toward the house, but then I pause when I see a familiar face heading my way from the opposite direction.

The two of us meet halfway, at the bottom of Jerry's driveway, each mirroring the other's confused glance.

"Tony," I say, "what are you doing here?"

"Ey, Will. I was about to ask you the same." His black mustache twitches. Instead of his usual gray jumpsuit, he wears a hooded sweatshirt and jeans.

"I asked you first," I insist.

"Fair 'nough. The old man closed the shop today because of what happened to Jerry. Except I don't think it was an accident. I think someone did it to him. I aim to figure out who."

"Oh," I say, somewhat surprised. "Did Sammy ask you to do it?"

"Sammy? Heck, no. I just want to know who killed my pal." He looks me over and adds, "Your turn."

"Okay. I agree that it doesn't seem like an accident, and I'm also looking into who killed Jerry."

"Why?" He narrows his eyes at me and asks, "Did Sammy ask *you* to do it?"

Obviously. "He did," I tell him. "They were good friends, him and Jerry."

Tony nods sadly. "I know."

"Do you know that the police took Garrett into custody?"

He nods again. "I heard. But to be honest, that feels…"

"Too easy?"

"Yeah."

"That's what I said."

Tony shakes his head. "I got a kid of my own around Garrett's age. He goes to school in New York. Can't imagine what Carla must be going through."

"So you came here to talk to her, see if she knows anything that could help?"

"Bingo. But since we're both here, maybe we should both go," Tony suggests.

"Uh… you know, maybe I should go in alone," I tell him. "Nothing personal, but sometimes you come off as a little… brusque."

He stiffens visibly. "Brusque? What are you talkin' about, brusque?" Then his shoulders slump a little and he mutters, "Okay,

I see what you mean. I'll wait out here; you'll tell me what she says?"

"Every word."

He nods. "You're a good pal, Will."

I force a smile and head up the driveway. People keep telling me that, but I don't always feel like it.

A BASKET OF MURDER: A PET SHOP MYSTERY BOOK FOUR

CHAPTER 7

Tony heads back to his truck, parked about a half-block in the opposite direction, and sits in the cab while I head up the walkway to talk to Carla. My finger is poised to ring the doorbell when the door swings open, and Carla—looking very surprised to see me—takes a step back.

"Will, what are you doing here?" Her eyes are red with dark bags beneath them; I'm guessing she didn't get much sleep last night, and has obviously been crying.

"I, uh, just wanted to stop by and express my condolences," I tell her. "About Jerry."

"That's very nice of you, but you'll have to wait for the funeral," she says. "I have to go down to the courthouse for Garrett's preliminary hearing and hope that the judge will set bail." She shakes her head. "He has priors, so I don't know what's going to happen."

"Um, can I ask what priors he has?"

She frowns. "Why?"

"Because…" Honesty is the best policy, isn't it? "Carla, let me be frank: I don't think Garrett did what they're saying he did."

"Why do you think that?" she asks candidly.

"Because… you know. He's just a kid. And to do that, and stick around the crime scene, I mean—he'd have to be a sociopath, wouldn't he?"

"So you don't think my son was responsible for Jerry's death, even though you don't know him, and you're… what, exactly? Investigating on your own?" She cranes her neck past me and asks, "And is that Tony's truck parked down there? What's he doing here?"

"I…"

"Listen, Will, I think it's nice of you to stop by, and even nicer to advocate on Garrett's part. But let's be real here. The only thing that's going to save him is finding hard evidence that it *wasn't* him." She sniffs once and adds, "It doesn't look good. Ever since me and his father divorced, he's been lashing out more and more. In the past year alone, he's been caught breaking and entering, underage drinking, and fighting. Each time, Patty's given him a slap on the wrists—but this is too big." She sniffs again and blinks back some tears. "You know, when I got home last night from my shift at the hospital and found Jerry, the first thing I did was call 911. The second thing I did was check the house for Garrett. He was sleeping in his room, and he had his music on. He hadn't heard a thing. But even when I told him what happened, his reaction was… how can I put it? It was lackluster." She shrugs. "He didn't like Jerry and I don't think he's upset that he's dead. That's not going to look good for him. Not at all."

"I'm really sorry, Carla."

She steps out onto the porch and locks the front door behind her. "I have to go." She strides past me, down the driveway and into her car.

After she pulls away, Tony gets out of his truck and joins me at the bottom of the driveway.

"So what'd she say?" he asks eagerly. "Does she know anything?"

"Nothing helpful," I tell him somberly. "Hey, Tony, let me ask you. Put yourself in Garrett's shoes for a second. Let's say you did it; you kicked the car and the jack tipped and crushed Jerry. What would you do?"

"Me?" He scoffs. "I'd be in North Dakota by now. I'd change my name to Sven and live in the mountains herding goats or something."

"Yeah. Me, too. Well, not the goats part, but I'd be as far away from here as I could. So why would he stick around then? That's not throwing any suspicion off of him."

"Doesn't add up."

"No, it doesn't. I'm not sure where I'm going to go with this next, but I'm invested now. I plan to see this through."

"I do, too," Tony says. "Hey, maybe we can divide and conquer. Share information and see if we can't figure this thing out together."

"Alright, deal," I agree. "If I find anything, I'll let you know."

"And I'll do the same." We shake on it.

As I'm heading back to my car, Tony calls out. "Oh, Will. You said you have a lawyer, right?"

I turn back, thrown by the question. "Huh?"

"Like, a business lawyer, to draft up contracts and stuff."

"Oh. Yeah, I do."

"Cool. Do you think you can put me in touch with him? I'm getting everything together for the franchise. With Jerry gone, I really don't think I can stay there much longer."

"Sure thing, Tony," I tell him. "Oh, and it's her."

"Her?"

"The lawyer, it's a her. I'll get you the number."

"Great. Thanks, Will."

*   *   *

Unsure of where to go next, I head back to the Pet Shop Stop. At least I can take a breather, bounce some ideas off of Sarah, and figure out what my next step should be. More than anything I just wish that Sammy would be more forthcoming with whatever he knows or thinks he knows. That's an angle to this mystery I haven't yet even begun to unravel: what's his part in all this?

I walk into the shop and let out a long, deflating sigh. Karen is there, chatting idly with Sarah near the counter. They both smile at me when I enter.

"Hi Will," Karen says.

"Hello, Karen." I don't even try to sound enthusiastic.

"I was just talking to Sarah about stealing her away from you for another night out next week," she adds. "Hope you don't mind."

"Not at all." I force a smile, reminding myself not to be petty. "Sarah, can I talk with you a moment?"

"Sure." We retreat to the back office, a tiny closet-like room that also serves as overstock space, so we have to stand almost nose-to-nose.

"I went and spoke with Carla," I tell her.

"Wait, before you say anything, I just want to tell you that you were right," she says.

"Right about what?"

"I understand that we can't keep Basket. We've got too much going on, and I know you're stressed already about possibly taking those classes, and we just don't need the added strain of a baby kitty."

"Wow. Thank you for understanding. I know it's not easy for you."

"That's why Karen is here," she admits. "I figured that maybe she could take Basket in; she adopted Pookie from us." She frowns. "Unfortunately, her apartment building only allows one pet."

"Oh. Well, we'll keep looking." I give her a reassuring hug.

"Okay. Now you go," she says.

"Right. So I went to talk with Carla Kunkle; it wasn't great. She thinks that Garrett is going to be charged unless the cops find evidence that it wasn't him."

"That's no good. Poor kid."

"And poor Carla. First Jerry, and now it looks like she might lose Garrett, too—"

"Carla Kunkle?" Karen asks from somewhere nearby.

I peer out of the tiny room to find Karen leaning against the wall, inspecting her fingernails.

"Are you eavesdropping?"

"Yeah, a little," she admits. "What's wrong with Carla? I just saw her last night."

"What do you mean, you saw her last night?"

"After me and Sarah left Holy Frijole, I stopped by Better Latte Than Never for a hot chocolate. I saw her there. She was with, uh, um, what's his name..." She snaps her fingers a few times. "Uh... Blake. Yeah."

"Blake... her ex-husband?" I ask.

"Yeah. Why? Is that weird?"

"Yes, Karen. That's weird," Sarah says, as she and I exchange a worried glance.

SUSIE GAYLE

CHAPTER 8

"So she was actually at the coffee shop," I tell Sammy excitedly, "when she said she was at the hospital finishing a shift!" I pace the barber shop floor. "And guess who she was there with."

"Her ex-husband?" he asks, sweeping dark hair into a small pile on the floor.

"Uh… yeah. How'd you know that?"

"I didn't know that. I just figured it was the most likely person, considering how you charged in here all jazzed up."

As soon as Karen delivered the news about spotting Carla last night, I had grabbed my coat and hurried down to the shop to tell Sammy about it. Luckily he has no customers at the moment; just the two retired regulars, Frank and Marcus, both of whom like to spend their afternoons sitting in the barber shop and listening to gossip (which is why I'm careful to avoid using names like "Carla" or "Jerry," just in case).

"Well, thanks for stealing my thunder," I tell Sammy. "But don't you see? That means she was lying about where she was—which could mean any number of things."

"Like maybe her and the ex were messing around behind Jerry's back? Maybe they were planning to get back together or something?" Sammy suggests. "But could that lead a person to do… that thing that happened?" He throws a furtive glance toward the retirees, who both pretend to read newspapers while they eavesdrop.

"I don't know," I admit. "And there's another problem with that theory: Why on earth would she let her son take the fall?" I shake my head. It doesn't make sense. If Carla or Blake had anything to do with Jerry's death, there's no way they'd try to pin it on their only child. "I just thought you should know about it," I tell Sammy. "I'm going to head to the coffee shop and see if I can't get any answers."

"Good idea." He looks up at the clock. "Huh. It's three. Normally on Fridays I'd be closing the shop early and heading to the rec center to play racquetball with Jerry."

"And I'll have to call Tony," I continue, pacing the shop floor. "He's doing his own thing parallel to mine; we promised to share info." Suddenly I look up and frown at Sammy. "That's the third time you've mentioned racquetball. What gives?"

He just shrugs. "I like racquetball."

I stare at him for a while. He stares blankly back.

"So there's nothing more you want to tell me?" I ask him.

"Nope."

I grunt in frustration. "Fine. I'll talk to you later."

*   *   *

I call Tony as I head over to the coffee shop and I tell him what I found out. He calls Carla a few choice words that make me wince.

"Hey, come on now," I say. "We don't know anything for sure."

"We know for sure that she lied, not only to us but to the cops, too," Tony counters.

"Okay, that's true."

"What do you want to bet that they were sneaking around on poor ol' Jer?"

"I don't want to bet anything. I want to find out the truth. I'm heading to the coffee shop now; I'll be in touch."

I hang up. This seems like my obvious next move, but I can't dismiss Sammy's cryptic mentions of racquetball. I've known him long enough that I should've realized he was trying to tell me something the first time he brought it up; any idiot could say the same after three times.

I enter Better Latte Than Never to find a bored-looking young woman managing the counter. She greets me halfheartedly and asks what I'd like.

"Good afternoon. I'd like to know who was working the closing shift last night."

"One moment," she mutters. Then she suddenly shouts, "Ham!"

A gawky kid with sandy hair comes out from the back room in a black apron with the shop's logo on it. He grins wide when he sees me. "Hey Will, long time no see!"

"Ham? You work here now?" Hammond Dobes is, as far as I'm aware, the bagger at the general store in town. He took a year off from school to save up for college. He and I have a bit of history on account of him nearly being accused of murder back in October.

"Oh, don't worry. I still work at Miller's," he assures me, as if my world would end if he wasn't bagging my groceries every Sunday. "I picked up some part-time shifts here to save more money."

"Great," I tell him. "Listen, did you close the shop last night?"

"Sure did. Why?"

"There was a couple here. A woman with dark hair, probably in nurse's scrubs, and—"

"And a tall guy with blond hair? Yeah. They were here." He rolls his eyes. "They were here almost all night."

"They were?"

He nods. "We're supposed to close at eleven, but those two stayed until almost midnight," he says. "I tried to tell them I had to lock up, but they were in a pretty heated conversation. I didn't want to get in the middle of it."

"You're absolutely certain they were both here that late?" I ask.

"Definitely. They left about two minutes before I did. You can check my time card."

"No, that's okay, Ham. Thanks. Uh… any idea what they were talking about?"

"I was mostly trying to avoid them, but they were definitely blaming each other for something. They kept saying 'he,' so I guess they were talking about a guy—maybe a son? And then they argued about money for a while."

"Okay. Thanks, Ham." I head out of the coffee shop. That didn't really help much; in fact, I'm right back to square one. Carla and Blake might have been meeting secretly, but they have an airtight alibi for the time of Jerry's death.

I get back into my car and drum on the steering wheel for a while. *Think, Will.* The most logical thing to do would be to call Patty and tell her that Carla lied… but what good would that do? Carla obviously didn't kill Jerry, and Patty might arrest her for falsifying her story. Then there's the racquetball thing. What is Sammy trying to tell me? I suppose the rec center is the next obvious step—either that or talking to Carla again to confront her about the lie.

I turn the key in the ignition and the engine turns over. Then it chugs once, twice, and dies. Great. Just what I need.

SUSIE GAYLE

CHAPTER 9

My baby, my darling, one of the great loves of my life, she just won't start again. If that sounds melodramatic, it just means that you've never owned a reliable car for nine years. My SUV never once broke down on me or left me stranded. I always keep her in the best working order I can, but I suppose time and tide wait for no sport utility vehicle.

After three more fruitless attempts, I give up on trying and instead just sit there, pouting, for about two solid minutes before I realize something.

I know a guy.

I call Tony. "Listen, I do have new information," I tell him, "but more important right now is that my car just died."

"Oh, bummer. Where are you?"

"Outside Better Latte Than Never. I know you're off-duty today, but…"

"Ey, say no more. The old man won't mind if I borrow the tow truck. I'll be there in no time and we'll get you straightened right out."

I breathe a sigh of relief. "Thank you."

True to his word, Tony arrives about fifteen minutes later. He pops my hood and pokes around for a short while, then lowers it and wipes his hands on his sweatshirt.

"Looks like your starter crapped out on you," he tells me. "Fairly easy fix."

"Good, good." I look down at the road sheepishly and ask, "Uh, how much is that going to cost?"

"Ordinarily? Parts, labor, towing… all in you'd be looking at around six-fifty, seven hundred." My eyes must pop out of my head, because he quickly adds, "But you're a friend. I'll do it in my downtime and just charge you for parts—it'll be around two hundred."

"Whew. Wow. Thank you, Tony. That's… really, really generous of you."

"No problem. Just don't tell the old man. Our little secret, okay?"

"You got it."

Tony rigs my baby to the back of the truck and hoists it up onto the flatbed. "I'm going to take this back to the shop. I'll call you when it's done; it'll probably be Monday, Tuesday at the latest. You okay? You got a ride from here?"

"I'll call someone. Thanks again."

He gives me a little salute and gets back into the tow truck. I watch him haul my beautiful car away, and then I take out my phone and call Sarah to tell her what happened.

"I can close the shop for a few minutes to come get you," she says.

"I don't need to come to the shop. I need to get over to Carla's and see why she lied to the police, and then go to the rec center and see what's so oddly interesting about racquetball."

"I'm sorry, Will. One of us is going to have to stay here; we can't just close the store so we can run around investigating."

"You're right." See? She's far more responsible than I am. I would indeed just close the shop and go run around investigating. "Then can I borrow your car?"

There is a long, pregnant pause on the other line.

"Sarah? Hello?"

"I'm here. Um… I'm kind of weird about other people driving my car. I mean, you're not on my insurance. What if something happens?"

"Sarah Jane! Do you not trust me?" I ask incredulously.

"Oh! Wait. I have a solution," she says suddenly. "Let me make a quick call."

*   *   *

I fold my arms across my chest and scowl as a hunter green sedan pulls up to the curb in front of me about ten minutes later. The passenger side window whirs down slowly and Karen leans across the seat to grin up at me.

"Hey," she says. "Hop in, stranger."

Reluctantly, I get in the car. It seems that Sarah's "solution" was that Karen took the day off today and could be my personal chauffeur—the idea of which apparently thrilled the latter.

"Maybe this can be an opportunity," Sarah had said, "for you to see that she's not the same person she was when you were married."

(To which I had grumbled, "I don't *wanna* see if she's not the same person she was when we were married," because I'm a mature adult.)

"Alright, meter's running," Karen says. "Just kidding. Where to?"

"Uh… I guess the first stop would be Jerry Brahms' house. You know where that is?"

"Sure do." She pulls away from the curb. We drive in silence for a minute or so, and then she asks, "So, you think Carla might have done it?"

"Done what?" I say innocently.

"Come on, Will. Sarah told me all about your little investigation into Jerry's death."

I groan. It seems Sarah and I will have to talk about what's considered a private conversation.

"Hey, if you want to bounce some ideas off me, I'm game," Karen says. "Tell me what you've got so far."

"I'd rather not," I mutter, staring out the window.

"Hey, Mr. Pouty-Face, listen. I know you don't like me and Sarah being friends, but the truth is, I like her—and I see why you like her. She's a nice woman. The harder truth is, you don't get to say who either of us can be friends with."

"But that doesn't mean I have to like it."

"No, I guess you don't. But maybe if you gave me a chance, you'd see that I'm working pretty hard on the whole self-improvement thing." She pauses for a long moment and adds, "Did you ever stop to think that maybe it's not so easy for me to see you this happy with someone else?"

Her question takes me off guard. I glance over at her, but she stares blankly ahead at the road.

"No," I murmur. "I guess I didn't think about that."

"Well, it's not."

"I'm... sorry."

"It's okay. Don't you worry; as soon as I find my rich, smokin' hot Mr. Right, I plan to rub your nose all up in it."

I can't help but laugh a little. "Alright. Deal."

SUSIE GAYLE

CHAPTER 10

Karen slows the car as we pass by Jerry's house, just as I asked her to, but Carla's car isn't there. I was afraid of that, that she might still be out attending Garrett's preliminary hearing.

"Alright, we'll have to come back," I tell her.

"Then where to next?"

"Let's head to the rec center."

She frowns. "The rec center? Why?"

Regardless of whether or not I'm able to trust Karen, I certainly don't want to tell her about Sammy's possible involvement in this whole mess. "Just playing a hunch."

She shrugs and turns up a side street. "So what makes you think it could be Carla?" she asks me.

"Truth be told, I don't think it was Carla. Her alibi checks out; problem is, it's not the same alibi she gave to me or the police."

"And you want to know why?"

"Yup."

She thinks for a moment. "What if Carla and Blake *wanted* to be seen?"

"Huh?"

"Well, they were in pretty public venue, and when I saw them, they were arguing. Chances are good other people noticed that, too," she says. "What if they wanted to be seen there… so that someone else could kill Jerry and they wouldn't take any blame?"

"What… do you mean like they hired someone to do it? Jeez, Karen, this isn't a movie."

She shrugs. "I'm just saying. If I wanted to kill someone, I wouldn't do it myself, and I'd make sure that I had a solid alibi."

I have to admit, it's not a bad thought. "But that doesn't explain why Carla would lie to the police. If she wanted to establish an alibi and went through all that trouble to be seen at the coffee shop, you would think she'd tell the truth about where she was."

"Hm. I guess you're right about that." She glances over at me and smiles. "Sarah was right. You are pretty good at this stuff."

"Thanks." I don't point out how often other people, like Sammy and Sarah, tend to help me along by thinking of things that I didn't.

The rec center is a squat, L-shaped brick building adjacent to the public park. Though I've only been inside a few times, I know they have an indoor swimming pool, a basketball court, shuffleboard, and at least one, if not more, racquetball courts.

Karen pulls the car into an empty spot in the front row of the lot. There are only a handful of cars, considering it's just after four o'clock on a weekday.

"You're not going to tell me why we're here, are you?"

"Nope, sorry." I get out and Karen follows me inside, where we're greeted by a young woman at a reception desk with a plastic name tag that says "Melissa."

"Hi! Welcome. Can I help you with something?" she asks brightly.

"Yes, actually you can, Melissa," I tell her. "Is the racquetball court reserved?"

She sticks out her lower lip as she consults a clipboard on her desk. "Normally the court is reserved weekly at this time, but… looks like that's been cancelled, so it's available. Can I set you up with it?"

"No, no. Um… the names on the reservation, they were Jerry Brahms and Sam Barstow, right?"

"Actually, yes, they were," the girl says. She frowns at me with her eyes while still smiling politely.

"Was there anyone else on that reservation?"

She shakes her head. "No, just the two of them."

"What about the other facilities? Any reservations on any of those for the same time?"

This Melissa frowns with her whole face. "What's this in regards to?"

"Please, it's important," I tell her.

"Uh... I'm sorry. I don't think I can share that with you."

"Alright. Thanks anyway." I start to turn away, but Karen shoots me a look of incredulity, as if to say, *That's it?*

She puts her palms on the desk and leans forward, only inches from Melissa's face. The younger woman leans back, perturbed. "Listen here, *Melissa*," Karen says quietly. "I don't know if you heard, but Jerry Brahms was found dead last night."

"Oh my goodness!" Melissa's hand flies to her mouth. "I didn't know... gosh, he came in here every week!"

"I know. It's terribly sad. And the police, they suspect foul play. Now my friend here," she gestures toward me with her head, "for some nutty reason, thinks that the information you have on your little clipboard there could help. So why don't you take another look-see, huh?"

I almost laugh at Karen's threatening demeanor—she's only five-three in heels—but then I remember how many times during our marriage she scared the bejesus out of me.

Poor Melissa looks close to tears. She looks upward toward the ceiling. I follow her gaze; there's a security camera mounted in the corner, trained on the front desk and, at the moment, us.

"I'm really, *really* sorry," she says, "but I can't tell you. I could lose my job."

Karen scoffs. "Fine, be that way. But you might be letting a murderer go free—"

"Come on, Karen," I say gently.

"Some crazed killer out there, you're just gonna let him slide—"

"Karen, let's *go*." I take her gently by the arm and we head toward the door.

"What would Jerry think, Melissa?" she shouts as we leave. Outside, she continues her rant. "The nerve of that girl! Like giving us a name would be the end of the world—"

"Wait!" We both turn to see Melissa running after us across the parking lot. "Wait. I couldn't say anything in there because the cameras have an audio feed. Jerry and Sam were the only two on the reservation, but they've been coming here every Friday for about two years now, and they used to have a third—Tom Savage."

"Tom Savage," I repeat. "The used car dealer?"

"The guy with those super annoying radio commercials?" Karen adds.

"Yeah, him. He used to come every week, but about four months ago or so, he stopped coming. I don't know if that means anything. I hope it helps." She turns and trots back into the rec center.

Karen and I exchange a glance. "You're the expert here. Does that mean anything?"

I shrug. "Trust me, I'm no expert, and I have no idea. But I think we ought to go pay Mr. Savage a visit and see why he stopped coming."

We get back in Karen's car and pull out of the parking lot.

"Huh," I say aloud.

"What?"

"Nothing, I just… I didn't know three people could play racquetball, that's all."

Karen scoffs at me.

A BASKET OF MURDER: A PET SHOP MYSTERY BOOK FOUR

CHAPTER 11

On the way to Savage Cars, I give Sammy a call from my cell phone to share with him my new findings—or at least that's my intention.

"I'm on my way to see Tom Savage," I tell him.

"Good. Tell him I said hi," he replies, and hangs up. I stare at the phone in confusion for a long moment, and then call Sarah.

"Tom Savage?" she says. "He's on the Seaview Rock town council."

"He is?"

"Yes, Will. You know, it wouldn't hurt for you to be a little more active locally, especially as a business owner—"

"Sarah."

"Right, sorry. Um, if I remember correctly, he introduced the downtown revitalization plan."

"…The what plan?"

She sighs. "The downtown revitalization plan. It's an outline to fix roads, fill in potholes, install new parking meters… stuff like that. He's spearheading the whole thing."

"So… he's a good guy?"

"Yeah, I mean, as far as the town's concerned he is. I think I recall that he's putting a chunk of his own money into it, too."

"Thanks. I'll let you know how it goes." I end the call and say to Karen, "So Sarah tells me that Savage is—"

My cell phone rings, interrupting me. It's Tony.

"Ey, Will. Just wanted to let you know that I ordered the part we need for your car. It'll be here Monday, and I'll drop it in then. Bada-bing, done."

"Oh, thanks Tony. You're a lifesaver."

"No sweat. Listen, you mentioned an accountant, too. You think you can pass along a number for him—or her—when you get the chance?"

"Sure thing, Tony. It would be the least I can do."

"Great."

"Um… by the way, how's it going on your end, with the Jerry thing?"

He sighs. "Truth be told, between your car breaking down and the old man grieving over Jer, I haven't had any time. Casey is really broken up about it; Jerry worked here for almost twenty years."

"I know. Well, I'm on my way to talk to someone; I'll let you know if anything pans out."

"Yeah, please do. Talk soon." Nothing personal against Tony, but since I have no idea what Sammy and Jerry have to do with Tom Savage, I'm not going to go throwing any accusations around.

"Who was that?" Karen asks.

"Tony, my mechanic. He's giving me a real good deal to fix my car."

"Tony from Sockets & Sprockets?"

"Yeah. You know him?"

"I do," she admits. "He told me he'd give me a 'good deal' a couple months ago when I needed new tires."

"Huh. Maybe he's just a real nice guy."

She snorts. "Yeah. Nice guy. He told me it was because I was a 'pretty little thing,' and that he hoped to 'see a lot more of me soon.'"

"Oh. Well, maybe he's just a nice guy *and* a big flirt." I didn't peg Tony as that kind of guy; he always seemed to me to be devoted to his wife.

"Sure… except that the next day, he came into the bank to make a deposit, and he saw me there. Asked me to go for drinks with him. I turned him down politely, and he goes and charges me full price for the work on my car."

"That's… kind of sleazy," I admit. "Especially since the guy is married."

Then I bite my lip, because for a moment I forgot who I was riding in the car with—the then-Jezebel that ran off with Portland Guy and ended our marriage.

She realizes it too, and we drive in silence for what feels like an eternity and is easily the most awkward silence I've ever been a part of.

"Sorry," I mutter eventually. "I didn't mean it like that. I'm not, like, still bitter or anything—"

Karen clears her throat loudly. "So!" she exclaims. "How are we going to handle this chat with Tom Savage?"

I breathe a short sigh of relief, glad for the change of topic. "Well, I thought we'd start by asking why he stopped coming to play racquetball with those guys, and then see where that takes us, and…"

I trail off because Karen groans loudly. "Will, you're too soft. No offense. You're not going to get answers by asking politely. No one's going to be like, 'Oh, yeah, I totally killed Jerry.' Grab the bull by the horns! March in there, and demand answers! Assert dominance! Isn't that what you do with dogs?"

"Well, some people prescribe to that type of training, but personally I don't think it's all that helpful—"

"Trust me, it works on people. Walk in there like you know something you don't. If he thinks you do, he just might cave."

"You really think that will work?"

"You'll only know by trying."

Assert dominance. Pretend I know something I don't. Sure, easy.

"You know," I tell her, "for someone working on self-improvement, you're still really pushy."

SUSIE GAYLE

"One thing at a time, Will. One thing at a time."

A BASKET OF MURDER: A PET SHOP MYSTERY BOOK FOUR

CHAPTER 12

I hype myself up a bit before we head inside the building that houses the offices of Savage Cars. I take a few deep breaths, and then I puff out my chest and hold my head high. Karen follows behind me as I march inside and demand to see Tom Savage.

"I'm sorry, sir, he's in a meeting," the wide-eyed receptionist tells me.

"He's *about* to be in a meeting!" I announce boldly.

"Yeah!" Karen backs me up.

"With me!" I feel kind of silly, but I stand my ground. That is, until I realize I've never been here before. "Uh… which one's his office?"

Karen points. "I'm guessing it's the one that says 'Tom Savage, Owner and CEO' on the door."

"Right. Good catch." I stride over to the door and throw it open.

Behind a wide oak desk, a portly fellow in a beige suit looks up in alarm, cradling a phone receiver to his ear.

"Um, hello," he says, confused. "Can I help you?"

"Hi, Tom. Sammy Barstow says hi. Jerry Brahms would too, but he's dead." Wow. Did that just come out of my mouth?

Tom Savage's eyes widen to the point of falling out. "I'll… call you back," he says into the phone, and then slowly lowers it to its cradle. "Alright," he says cautiously, "let's talk. Privately." He says the last part while eyeing up Karen.

"Fine. I'll wait outside," she mutters, closing the door behind her.

Tom Savage stays seated and eyes me up for a long moment. "I know you," he says eventually. "You run the pet shop, right?"

"That's right."

"And you're tight with the barber."

"You mean Sam? Yes."

Tom nods slowly, as if putting something together in his mind that I have no idea about. He gestures to an empty chair. "Would you like to have a seat?"

"I'd like to know why Jerry is dead."

"Hey now…" Tom puts both his hands up in a defensive gesture. "Come on. I had nothing to do with that."

"No? You sure about that, Tom?"

"For god's sake, why would I? I'm getting what I want, and they're getting what they want. It's a win-win. I mean, it's blackmail, but it's still win-win. And I have to admit, it's great for the town—and my image. I had nothing to gain from getting rid of Jerry."

Okay, now I *really* have no idea what he's talking about, and I'm finding it hard to keep up my tough-guy persona with terms like "blackmail" and talk of premeditated murder.

"Alright, Savage," I tell him, trying to keep my voice steady. "I believe you."

He sighs with relief. "So are you in on this too now?" he asks. "You're not going to start making demands of me, are you?"

"No, I'm not. But we'll be watching you."

"Yeah. Of course," he murmurs. "Thanks."

I retreat toward the door, but he calls out to me again. "Wait a sec, hey. You know animals, right?"

"Yeah…"

"Can you tell me what's wrong with my snake?"

"Your… snake?" I turn slowly to see that Tom is pointing out a small glass enclosure on a side table that I hadn't noticed before, what with all my barging in and throwing around accusations.

"Yeah. She's not eating lately. I think something's wrong with her."

I approach the glass cage very, very cautiously, as if the creature within it will suddenly burst out. Inside, coiled in some sand, is a snake about two feet long, with a spade-shaped head and olive markings.

"Tom," I say slowly, "that is a tiger rattlesnake. Its venom has the highest toxicity of any snake in the United States."

He grins. "I know. Isn't she beautiful?"

"But... why... do... you... *have*... that?"

He shrugs. "I like snakes. Don't worry, I don't handle her. I just like watching her. But like I said, she won't eat lately, and the nearest vet that handles snakes is in the city."

"I can't help you," I tell him, backing away from the cage. The snake lifts its head and stares at me, its black tongue flicking between its jaws. My blood runs cold. "I have to go. Sorry." Even just seeing the snake through the glass gives me the heebie-jeebies.

I hurry out to find Karen sitting in the waiting area, flipping through a magazine. She tosses it aside when she sees me.

"Well? How'd it go?"

"It's not him," I say quickly, without stopping.

"No? How can you be sure?"

"I'm sure."

"Then why did he stop playing racquetball with those guys?" she asks, following me quickly.

"Too busy."

She shoots me a lopsided, confused glance, but unlocks the car and doesn't push the issue. Once we're back in the car, Karen grins. "So, how'd that feel, taking charge?"

"Not great," I admit. "It felt kind of...dirty. It's just not me."

She shrugs. "But you got the answers you were looking for."

Yeah, I think. *And then some.* As much as I want to know what Sammy is into with Savage, I don't think I'm quite ready to have that conversation just yet. Like Karen said, one thing at a time—and the thing at this time is still to discover who committed the murder.

Instead I tell her, "Let's head back over to Jerry's house and see if Carla's home."

A BASKET OF MURDER: A PET SHOP MYSTERY BOOK FOUR

CHAPTER 13

Karen eases the car to a stop at the curb outside Jerry's house at the same time that Carla's car pulls into the driveway. She gets out, sees me in the passenger seat, and puts her hands on her hips, looking unhappy and impatient.

"Stay here," I tell Karen. "Let me handle this." No offense to Karen, but she can be a tad gruff and I don't want to push Carla's buttons.

I get out and put on a big smile as I head up the driveway. "Hi, Carla."

"What do you want, Will?"

"I, uh…" Is there a friendly way to accuse someone of lying to the police? "Well, some new information has come to light, and I thought you might want to know. By the way, how did things go for Garrett?"

She shakes her head and looks up. "The judge denied him bail, so my son gets to sit in jail until his arraignment. As you can probably guess, I'm having what is likely the worst twenty-four hours of my life, so please don't take this the wrong way, but unless you have something that can help Garrett, I'd really like to be alone right now."

Even though she's being curt, I notice a small glimmer of hope in her eye that maybe I brought some good news.

"I'm sorry. I'm not any closer to figuring it out."

"Then why are you here?"

Well, it's now or never, I guess. "Carla, I know that you were with Blake at the coffee shop last night."

Her gaze immediately turns hard and angry. "So?"

"So, that means that you lied to the police, and to me. I'd just... like to know why."

She sticks a finger in my face. "That is *none* of your business." Carla turns on a heel and strides toward the house.

Jeez. The woman just lost her significant other, and might lose her son too, and here I am threatening her. But still... if there was even the slightest chance that she or Blake was involved, I wouldn't be doing any justice by not pushing the issue. Grab the bull, right?

I take a deep breath and call after her, "The police would probably be interested to know that."

She stops. "Are you trying to intimidate me, Will?"

"No. I just want the truth," I tell her honestly.

She folds her arms and the scowl never leaves her face, but she motions toward the house with a jerk of her head. "Come in."

"Alright." I hold up a hand to Karen to signal, *five minutes*, and then I follow Carla up the walkway, into the living room she shared with Jerry. She shrugs out of her coat and takes off her shoes before saying another word to me.

"Are you going to tell the police on me?" she asks finally.

I shake my head. "Not unless there's reason to believe it's important to Jerry's case."

"I had nothing to do with it. Honest to God." Her eyes blur with the threat of tears. She blinks them back and motions for me to sit on the couch, and then takes a seat in an armchair facing me.

"You're right. I told Jerry that I was working a late shift at the hospital, but Blake and I did meet last night. We were discussing what to do about our son. Ever since the divorce, Garrett has been acting out, and getting worse. I suggested we send him to talk with a therapist, but it's expensive. I told Blake that if he cared about his son, we should split the cost. Blake insisted that Garrett didn't need therapy, and refused to pay for any of it." She shakes her head. "The deadbeat. Ever since Garrett turned eighteen, Blake's been off the hook for child support. He hasn't lent a dime."

"Okay," I say slowly. "Then why lie to the police about it?"

She sighs. "At first it was just my knee-jerk reaction. I'd already lied to Jerry about it, so I stuck with my story. I thought about telling them the truth afterwards, but I realized it might throw suspicion on me—I mean, meeting with my ex-husband the same night? You know what people would assume."

Yeah, I do know, considering the thought crossed my mind—not to mention Tony's and Karen's, too.

"But… why lie to Jerry about it in the first place?" I ask her. "If you were really meeting for Garrett's sake, don't you think Jerry would have understood?"

She nods. "Yeah, he would have. He was a good man. But I just didn't want him to worry any more than he already was."

"What do you mean, worrying more?" That's news to me—Jerry seemed to have it all together. "What was he worried about?"

"I'm not sure. He wouldn't talk to me about it. If I asked, he'd just say, 'it's nothing, it's nothing.' I know it wasn't money; we got by just fine. I think it had something to do with Mr. Casey."

"Why do you think that?"

"I heard him muttering in the garage one day, something about 'the old man.' That's what they call him, right?"

"Yeah, they do. Do you think Mr. Casey is sick or something?" Considering that he's looking to franchise Sockets & Sprockets, it could be that he wants to grow his legacy before he kicks the bucket.

Carla shrugs. "Like I said, I don't know."

"Just one more question. Did Jerry ever mention the name Tom Savage to you?" I'm just playing a hunch, but maybe whatever had Jerry so worried had something to do with the underhanded deal he had with Savage.

"The car guy from the radio?" She shakes her head. "I think Jerry used to see him at the rec center, but he hadn't mentioned him in months."

"Okay." Well, so much for my hunch. "Thank you, Carla. I'll leave you alone now. But if you need anything, anything at all, I hope you'll give me a call."

"Thanks, Will. And if you find anything out… please, do the same."

"I will."

I head back outside and get into the car, thinking.

"How'd that go?" Karen asks.

I give her the brief rundown of our conversation.

"So Jerry knew something about Mr. Casey that had him worried," Karen recaps. "What do you think it could be? And more importantly, do you really think that old man has it in him to tip a car?"

I shake my head. "No, I don't think Mr. Casey did this… but I think whatever had Jerry worried might be a good thing to know. Let's see if we can't find the old man."

A BASKET OF MURDER: A PET SHOP MYSTERY BOOK FOUR

CHAPTER 14

The Casey family has had roots in Seaview Rock since before it was even called Seaview Rock. One of Barton Casey's ancestors was a partner in a fish hatchery that opened here and was partially responsible for the boom into what is our present-day town. Eventually they sold their shares, and these days they own and operate a gas station, the auto body shop, and a couple of other local business. The old man only runs Sockets & Sprockets; he leaves the other business interests to his kids (which is a weird thing to say, considering they're all older than I am).

The Casey house is a huge colonial-style building up on the hill, which really isn't a hill at all but just the area that us locals call the ritzy part of town where the wealthy folk live. We head up there first and ring the doorbell, but no one answers.

After failing there, we decide to head down to Sockets & Sprockets. Sure enough, Mr. Casey's sleek black Lincoln is one of two cars in the lot—the other one being my dormant SUV. The sign on the door to the shop says "Closed," but I give it a little tug and find it's unlocked.

"Should we just… go inside?" I ask.

Karen rolls her eyes and pulls the door open. A bell chimes somewhere inside; a moment later Mr. Casey hobbles out from a rear office and frowns at us. He's pushing seventy, almost completely bald, and uses a cane to help him get around.

"Sorry, we're closed today," he says hoarsely.

"We know, Mr. Casey. Sorry to intrude like this. We just want to ask you a couple of questions, if we may, about Jerry Brahms."

His frown deepens, the wrinkles in his face pinching together. "About Jerry? Why? Who are you?"

Karen and I exchange an uneasy glance. I shake my head at her, just a little bit. There won't be any grabbing bulls by horns here. "Mr. Casey, maybe we can all have a seat and chat," I suggest. "Please. It's important."

"Well… alright." He motions for us to follow him into the rear office, where he settles into a comfortable-looking leather chair while Karen and I take seats in the pair of guest chairs on the other side of the desk.

"Mr. Casey," I begin, "I know this is going to sound harsh, but we have reason to believe that Jerry was… murdered."

The old man nods gravely. "I know. Tony told me about that boy getting arrested." He shakes his head. "Kids these days. They just do whatever they please, don't they? Poor Jer. He was the best mechanic I ever met."

"Then Tony must have also told you that we don't believe that Garrett did it."

Mr. Casey's brow furrows, his caterpillar-like eyebrows nearly meeting in the center. "No. Tony said he's certain the boy is guilty. That kid of Carla's always hated Jerry."

I exchange a nervous glance with Karen.

"Um, speaking of Carla," I say, "she told me that Jerry's been worried lately, but wouldn't tell her why. Would you happen to know why, Mr. Casey?"

The old man sighs. "Truth be told, the shop hasn't been doing so well," he admits. "That's why I want to franchise. If this location goes under, it'll be the end of Sockets & Sprockets."

"Franchise?" Karen says. "That's the first I'm hearing about this."

Mr. Casey's cell phone rings from atop the desk. He picks it up and squints at the screen, and then turns it towards us. "My eyes aren't what they used to be. Who's calling?"

I lean forward. "It's Tony."

"Ah. Give me one moment." He answers the phone. "Tony, my boy! Uh-huh. Sounds great. Sure. I'm just sitting here at the shop, talking with…" He cups the speaker and asks me, "What's your name again?"

"Will Sullivan."

"Will Sullivan," he tells Tony. "Yes, about poor Jerry. Okay then, see you soon." He ends the call. "Tony was scoping out a new location in Langford, about a half hour from here. He told me that you should stick around; he's on his way back and wants to talk with you."

"Wait," Karen says suddenly. "Tony is the one franchising the shop?"

"Of course," Mr. Casey tells us. "I don't want some random investor that's only looking to make a quick buck. I need someone I can trust; someone that knows the business."

"Mr. Casey, how long have you been working on the franchise deal?" she asks.

"Oh... almost two years now, I think. But we're finally ready. We plan to sign the paperwork before the end of the week."

I can tell that gears are turning in Karen's head, but whatever she's thinking she's not willing to say openly. Instead she stands and says, "I'm just going to use your restroom, if you don't mind."

"By all means," Mr. Casey tells her.

"Will, why don't you keep Mr. Casey company for a few minutes?" She briefly widens her eyes at me, the signal for *I'm not really going to use the bathroom.*

"Sure." She leaves the office. I smile awkwardly at Mr. Casey, unsure of where to go from here.

"So, Will, what do you do?" he asks.

"I own a pet shop downtown."

"Ah, a fellow entrepreneur! Wonderful. Tell me, have you ever thought about franchising? See, here's how it works..." He launches into an explanation of the finer points of expanding your business while I smile and nod. Franchising is definitively not my style; in fact, I've turned down more than one offer to sell the pet shop to large corporations. But hey, to each their own, I suppose.

My cell phone chimes in my pocket. It's a text, from an unknown number. It says, *Ask him who does his bookkeeping.* For a moment I'm terribly confused, until I remember that I don't have Karen's number in my phone anymore. She's texting me from elsewhere in the shop.

"Uh, Mr. Casey, to be honest, I'm not terribly interested in franchising," I tell him as politely as possible. He frowns a bit. "However, I am in the market for a new accountant. Who does your bookkeeping?"

"Oh, can't help you there," he says. "I do all the accounting myself."

"Ah. I see." Under the desk, I text her back. *He does.*

My phone chimes almost immediately. *Come here a sec.*

"Wouldn't you know it?" I tell the old man. "Now I have to use the bathroom. Too much coffee. Back in a flash."

I leave the office and find Karen in the reception area of the shop, click-clacking away on a computer with a POS system attached.

"What are you doing?" I whisper to her.

"Come here, look at this." She points to the screen. "They track their customers by last name, so naturally, I searched for myself." Sure enough, on the screen is an invoice for Bear, Karen.

"Okay, great. What does it mean?"

"Remember when I told you that Tony offered me a deal, and then charged me full price when I rejected him?"

"Yeah…"

"Well, look at the total that's marked here. He put me in the system under his original deal."

"So… you think that he pocketed the difference?"

"I think it's more complicated than that," she says gravely.

SUSIE GAYLE

CHAPTER 15

Tony arrives back at the shop about half an hour later. When he comes in, I'm waiting for him in the reception area. He greets me with a big smile.

"Ey, Will! Man, I just found the perfect location to open a shop. I can't wait to tell the old man all about it."

"Glad to hear it, Tony."

"And I'm glad you stuck around. I wanted to know if you found anything else about poor Jerry."

"As a matter of fact, I have."

"Well? Lay it on me."

Okay. Deep breath. Grab the bull. Assert dominance.

"For starters, I found out that it would cost at least fifty grand, if not more, for you to franchise a Sockets & Sprockets."

His smile dissipates. "Yeah, that's about right. So what?"

"I also know that you never applied for a loan through your bank—my ex-wife happens to be their loan officer."

"I didn't need to," he says somewhat defensively. "I saved up."

"Right—except that Mr. Casey told us he's been working on the franchise deal for about two years, which means that you couldn't have known about it before that. So are we to believe that you saved fifty thousand dollars in two years?"

"Well... of course not. I pulled some money from my retirement fund, 401K, savings account, all that jazz."

"That stands up to reason," I admit. "But there's one other thing. You charged a customer full price for a job, and then only logged a fraction of it into the system. Mr. Casey does all the bookkeeping himself, and his eyes aren't what they used to be. I'm guessing you pocketed the difference."

Tony frowns deeply. "Will, I don't think I like where this is going."

"I'm also guessing that's not the first or last time you've done it. It probably started small, doing favors for friends like you're doing for me. Then you realized you can get away with it, and upped the ante—charging full price and logging less."

Tony stares daggers at me for a long moment. "Alright. Fine, you got me. I've been skimming here and there. So what? In the end I'll open up another location and the old man will make all that money back anyway."

I shake my head. "He already knows, Tony."

The color drains from his face. "You... told on me?"

I nod. "He knows, and I think that Jerry knew, too."

Tony's mouth drops open a little. "No..."

"No? That's not what Jerry was worried about these past few months? I bet he knew you were skimming, but he was such a good friend that he didn't want to tell on you."

"No way…"

"He probably asked you to stop. Gave you the benefit of the doubt."

"That's not how it happened…"

"Maybe he gave you an ultimatum. Stop or he'll tell the old man. That night at the Runside, you had a few drinks, got bold. Decided to go visit Jerry later that night."

Tony shakes his head. "You don't know what you're talking about."

"He wasn't going to back down, though. So you got mad… and you kicked the car with him under it."

Tony shakes his head back and forth nervously, quickly. "No, no, no. See, maybe you can prove that I was skimming money off of jobs, but you can't prove anything about Jerry."

"See, that's where you're wrong. Turns out Jerry's neighbors have a surveillance system—cameras pointed at their front yard and curb. And those cameras caught your truck passing by right around the same time that the cops estimate Jerry was killed."

"They did?" he stammers.

I nod. "Yup." Okay, I should point out here that there are no surveillance cameras. That's me trying to get him to open up. But he doesn't know that. "And then Garrett was accused instead. See, you pretended to be interested in finding Jerry's killer, but really you were just trying to see if anyone would figure you out. And the only reason you're not in North Dakota, herding goats, is because you still had your opportunity to run your own shop."

Tony turns white as a sheet. "Who else knows about that? The cameras?"

"Only me."

"Okay. Okay, I can fix this. What do you want? You want money? I've got money. Let's say ten grand. I can get a loan for the difference. That's just for starters. Once I have the shop up and running, I'll give you ten percent if you never say a word. That could be a lot of money over your lifetime."

"I don't want your money, Tony." I'm surprised at how calm my voice sounds, because my heart is jackhammering in my chest. "I just want to know what happened to Jerry."

"It was an accident!" he hisses. "I kicked the car out of frustration, okay? It wasn't supposed to be that hard. It fell. I... I..." He takes a deep breath, on the verge of a panic attack. "Just take my deal, Will. Just take it!"

"I'm sorry, Tony. I can't."

From out of the back office, Mr. Casey hobbles out, his eyes brimming with tears. "Oh, Tony. How could you?"

Behind him, Karen comes out, followed by Chief Mayhew. Once Karen had discovered the discrepancy in the books, she shared her theory with me—the same one with which I just cornered Tony.

We checked out a few other customers of his and then called Patty right away.

Tony glances from one person to the next, his eyes finally drifting to the floor. His shoulders sag and he holds up his wrists, defeated.

SUSIE GAYLE

CHAPTER 16

Back at the Pet Shop Stop, Sarah looks from me to Karen and then back to me. "So when you really think about it," she says, "you didn't really solve this one, Will. Karen did."

"Well... I guess so," I admit.

"I would call it more of a joint effort," Karen says with a smile. "I wouldn't have even been involved without you, so let's share in the glory."

"Sure." I clear my throat. "Uh, and while I have you both here... I should apologize. I wasn't at all fair about the two of you having a relationship. It's not my place to tell either of you who you can be friends with, and if that's each other, then... I will be happy with that. Besides... it does seem like you've changed a lot," I tell Karen.

"Why thank you, Will," she says. "That's very mature of you—which means I guess you've changed a lot, too."

She grins. I roll my eyes.

"Well then," Sarah says, "how about to celebrate both a job well done and a new friendship, the three of us head down to the Runside and get some drinks?"

"Only if Will's buying," Karen says.

"Sure, why not." I can't help but grin. A lot can change in a short time, but obviously some things never will. "It's the least I can do for you carting me around all day."

"Speaking of, what are you going to do about your car now?" Sarah asks.

"Yeah," Karen adds, "you only knew two mechanics, and one sort of murdered the other."

"Actually, Mr. Casey said he was going to take care of it for me, free of charge, for helping him realize what a terrible mistake he was about to make."

"What?" Karen protests. "I did most of the work. What do I get out of it?"

"A swell of pride from knowing you did the right thing?" I suggest.

"And at least two martinis," she mutters. "I'll meet you two down at the Runside." She heads out the door, leaving Sarah and I to close up shop for the evening.

Once Karen is gone, Sarah says quietly, "I guess there's still that other thing though, huh?"

I nod. "Yes, there is still one other thing." I know without asking that she's referring to Sammy, and whatever reason he had for thinking that he could be a target.

I take Sarah's hand and look her right in the eye as I tell her, "Listen, I don't want to lie to you—ever. But we might have to agree that sometimes, there are things that I won't tell you. It might be for your own good, or it might be to protect a friend. You know that in my book, omitting is the same as lying, but… sometimes I might have to omit."

"I understand," she replies. "And sometimes I might be okay with you omitting those things, because it might alter my opinion of someone whose friendship I value."

"Thank you for understanding. Now I have to take a little walk—I'll be back in a few."

She nods as I head toward the door. I pause. "Just to be clear, we were just talking about me not telling you whatever reason Sammy had for thinking that he might be a target for murder and you being okay with it, right?"

"Yes."

"Good. Great. Okay, be right back."

*   *   *

The barber shop is closed by the time I get down there, but the lights are still on and through the window I can see Sammy sitting in his chair, waiting. I knock on the glass and he waves me inside.

"Lock the door," he tells me as I step in. I do so, and then I stand there awkwardly for a moment, considering how to start.

"You've always been the most honest guy I know," I say eventually. "You'll tell me when I need a haircut. You tell me when I'm being difficult or unfair. You're pretty much that way with everyone. It's one of the things we all like about you."

He nods slowly.

"You're also my best friend. I care about you and your wellbeing. When you said you thought you were a target, I did what I could."

"And I appreciate that."

"But it didn't turn out to be the way you thought it was. This was one of those cases when a simple solution was the right solution, and along the way I found out a few things that I kind of wish I hadn't. I can't just forget what I've heard, and I can't just keep it all in my head. So I'm going to talk, and you'll listen, and I don't want you to say anything. Okay?"

He nods again.

"Alright." I take a deep breath. "I think that while being racquetball buddies, you and Jerry discovered some kind of dirt on Tom Savage. Maybe he was embezzling money, or doing some kind of under-the-table deals. Maybe he's selling lemons. I don't know, and I don't want to know. But I think that instead of going to the authorities… the two of you blackmailed him. But not for personal gain; I think his downtown revitalization project was actually your idea. And it's a good idea. Businesses would do better, tourism would increase, and even though Savage could continue doing whatever it is he's doing, you would now have a town councilman in your pocket."

Sammy says nothing; he just stares at me stoically from his barber's chair, one hand resting on his chin.

"I think that when Jerry got killed, it freaked you out enough to ask for my help—but not enough to say anything that would incriminate you, even to me. All you did was guide me in the right direction, which was smart, because it turns out that Savage didn't have anything to do with Jerry, and I still don't know exactly what's going on. There's only one problem, and it's that Savage now thinks I'm a part of this. So I want to make it perfectly clear that I am not getting involved in any of this. I don't actually know anything, so I'm not going to go to Patty or tell anyone. But I don't want to know what's happening. I don't want to know about any demands that may or may not be placed on anyone else. I don't want to be involved. Period."

There's a long moment of silence, and then Sammy simply says, "Okay."

"Okay. Then… I guess I'll see you around." I turn to leave, but then I pause and face him again. "Look, I know you don't need a lecture from me, but blackmail is illegal, regardless of whom or what it might benefit. I know you well enough to know that you probably think you're doing the right thing, but part of you also knows it's wrong. And this whole ordeal should be a wake-up call for you. Maybe it's time to just put a stop to it."

Again Sammy just regards me evenly, not showing any sign of denial or confirmation. "Okay."

I head for the door once more, but behind me, Sammy speaks up.

"Will? They're right about you—Patty and Sarah and Karen. You would make a terrific investigator."

"Thanks, Sam. I'll see you later."

A BASKET OF MURDER: A PET SHOP MYSTERY BOOK FOUR

CHAPTER 17

I get back to the Pet Shop Stop and help Sarah with the closing duties. She can tell that I'm deep in thought, and I can tell that she really wants to ask about it, but neither of us says a word. Finally, when we're finished, I ask if she's ready to head down to the Runside.

"Sure. I think we could use a good drink after all this." She offers me a smile and a hug.

"You said it. Come on, Rowdy." Normally when I say that, I hear the telltale jingling of the tags on his collar as he jumps up from his bed and heads for the door, but this evening there's nothing. "Rowdy? Come on, boy."

I peer around the counter, behind which we keep his dog bed when he's hanging out with us in the shop. He lies on his side, curled up like a shrimp, and against his belly is Basket, the shop-cat.

"That is the most precious thing I have ever seen," Sarah says. "He loves Basket."

"That would be great, except that we're not keeping Basket," I remind her. "Come on, Rowdy. Kitty's going in a cage for the night." I reach down for the little gray cat, who looks up at me with his enormous blue eyes, and Rowdy... he *growls* at me.

Okay, maybe not so much a growl as a grunt of disapproval, but still enough to give me pause.

"Hey now," I scold. "None of that. We're not keeping the cat, Rowdy." I reach for the cat again, and Rowdy tightens his body against Basket. Then he licks my hand gingerly and stares up at me with his biggest, brownest puppy-dog eyes.

He whines a little. Basket yawns and punctuates it with a tiny squeak.

"Oh, come on, that's not fair."

"Will, I think Rowdy has adopted Basket," Sarah says beside me.

I sigh. "Fine. If you want to stay here with the kitten, then we'll go to the Runside without you."

Rowdy doesn't move. He just watches us, curled up against his tiny kitten friend.

Sarah puts her hand on my shoulder. "Let's just go, and we'll deal with this in the morning." I smile at her and shake my head; while I appreciate the sentiment, we both know that come morning, it'll be Rowdy and her against me... unless I change sides.

"I guess this will be the story we tell people about how we got a shop-cat," I mutter in surrender. "Alright, let's go."

I open the door and head outside and very nearly trip over a box just outside our door. "Oomph!" I cry out, staggering. "Jeez, what is with people leaving stuff outside our door?" I inspect the package. It's not a box, but rather a rectangular shape covered in a small brown blanket.

"What is it?" Sarah asks.

"I don't know. It looks like it could be a—ohmygod!" I pull off the blanket and then backpedal several feet, accidentally shoving Sarah aside in my effort to get back into the safety of the shop.

"Sheesh, Will, relax. It's just a snake." Sarah bends to inspect the olive-colored serpent inside the glass habitat.

It's not just any snake. It's the tiger rattlesnake from Tom Savage's office.

"We can't just leave it out in the cold. Let's bring it inside," she says.

"I'm not touching that thing, and it is *not* coming into my shop."

"Will… are you afraid of snakes?" A playful smile lights on her face, though I'm having trouble finding anything funny about the situation. I never told Sarah that I had a phobia about snakes—mostly because she never asked, but partially because even I have to admit that it's kind of weird for a pet shop owner to be afraid of something that most people consider a pet.

But let's be real here. Anyone who would willingly own one of those things is insane.

"Yes. I am afraid of snakes. I don't want it anywhere near—what are you doing?" I practically screech as Sarah lifts the glass cage and brings it inside.

"What would you rather me do? Leave it out there? Kill it? No way." She sets it down on the counter and peers inside. "It's kind of cool-looking."

"It is *not* cool. It is dangerous."

"Hey, there's a note taped to the top." She tears it off and opens it. "It says, 'Dear Will, consider this a small token of our newfound partnership. I hope that you will appreciate her as much as I did. She's still not eating properly, but I'm sure you can figure out why. Best regards, Tom Savage. P.S., her name is Petunia.'" Sarah glances up at me. "Newfound partnership? Is this one of those things we talked about earlier that I shouldn't ask about?"

"It most definitely is."

"I'm guessing he doesn't know you don't like snakes."

"That would be a good guess."

"Alright," Sarah shrugs. "Well, we'll leave her here tonight, and—"

"Figure out what to do in the morning?"

"Exactly. Come on, scaredy-cat." She leads me by an arm out of the shop. I glance mistrustfully at the snake over my shoulder until we're out the door again. I mean, who in their right mind would consider that a *gift*?

As we get into Sarah's car to head down to the Runside, another thought occurs to me, one far worse than a snake.

Maybe staying uninvolved in this blackmail scheme isn't going to be as easy as I thought.

SUSIE GAYLE

THE END

Printed in Poland
by Amazon Fulfillment
Poland Sp. z o.o., Wrocław